LOCKDOWN LUST

A collection of Steamy Stories from the 2020

Coronavirus Pandemic

By

Madison Berry

Table of Contents

One
Support System

"I really have to work."

It was impossible to understand how easily those words rolled off Anderson's lips as though he knew nothing of the emotional pain his rejection inflicted on me. But he did know. We had been married for three years after all, and had been in a relationship for two years before we said our wedding vows. That was enough time for him to know how bad body dysmorphia got me every time.

Sure, he was the head of the family and so he had to work. But we both knew that he never worked so late at night. There was no denying he was only trying to get away from me—the woman he'd been stuck with for the past three weeks without a way out.

We'd never spent so much time together; not since our honeymoon. Then again, we actually weren't spending much time together at the moment. It pretty much felt like Anderson still left home every morning to go to his office where he would spend no less than seven hours sitting at his desk. It didn't matter that he worked from home; I still felt his absence every single day, even more than I had prior to the damned corona virus pandemic.

When the virus struck hard and we were all made to stay safe and work from home, I had believed that this translated into more time with my husband.

But little did I know.

Anderson's words resounded in my head. *I really have to work.*

He had in no way sounded apologetic, and his face portrayed no such emotions. I would try to talk him into staying with me for a while, but that would mean giving him yet another chance to trigger my BDD.

He must have felt a tinge of guilt just as he turned to leave, and for a moment, I actually caught myself thinking he would reconsider and stay with me instead. He planted a kiss on my forehead and then he was gone, leaving me staring in the direction he had followed.

I plopped down on my bed with a defeated sigh. Three years ago, when I got married to Anderson, I'd never imagined thoughts of a possible infidelity would ever cross my mind. And now, it was the only reasonable explanation that could make me understand my husband's sickening attitude.

The blinking LED light on my smartphone directed my thoughts away from Anderson for a moment. I crawled across the bed to the other side where my phone sat idly on the drawer on the left side of the headboard.

Only a blind man would consider you fat. Those were the words of a total stranger to the emotionally broken woman I had become.

I had low-key forgotten that I had posted to a BDD support group on Facebook. A few days ago, I had attempted to wear a little black dress that had once been my favorite dress, but had remained unworn since I had our first child. But Anderson had remarked that I was too fat to fit into a UK size 8 dress. His thoughtless words had driven me to find comfort on social media, and now, as I read the comment a stranger posted barely a moment ago, a smile stretched my lips toward my ears.

I responded to his comment right away.

Me: *Thank you.*

He seemed to have been eagerly waiting for my response. His response came in just as soon as I sent out my reply to his initial comment.

My reply: *You're welcome. If you need someone to talk to, I'm just a text away.*

He probably didn't think I would—at least not so soon—but I accepted his invitation just as soon as he extended it to me. I needed someone to talk to anyway, just so I would not dwell on my husband's thoughtless choice of words. I visited the man's profile with the intention to only glance at his profile picture before messaging him.

The man appeared to be younger than I was. But that could probably be because he was clean-shaved, as opposed to Anderson's full beard which made gave off the feeling that he was already in his forties when he had just clocked thirty a few days ago.

The man's name was Malik. I had no idea where he came from, but he was the first Malik I had ever known. His eyes were a vibrant blue that seemed to stare into my soul the more I stared at the photo. I shuddered with the thought of just how intense his gaze would be if he were right in front of me, staring so deeply into my eyes. After I had stared long enough to take a mental picture of him, I initiated a conversation.

Me: *Hey (:*

Malik: *Hi*

My heart thumped. Once. Twice. Then once again. It suddenly seemed to forget how to beat normally. With each thump of my heart, there was a corresponding tightening of a knot in my stomach.

Malik's response was so swift I could swear he'd known I would not hesitate to message him. Was he as intrigued by me as I was by him? Had he also been checking out my profile? I wanted to believe the answers to these questions started with a 'y' but why should I be so inconsiderate to torture his poor vision with my unsightly body?

Sure, he'd seen a photo of me already, but his only comment was that I wasn't fat. I desperately wanted to believe that he liked what he saw, but a tiny voice in the back of my head told me that he was only being nice to stop me from sinking any deeper into depression.

Malik: *wanna be friends? (:*

Me: *Sure. (:*

Malik: *Thanks. It's pretty boring here. Needed someone new to talk to.*

Malik: *Dumb Rona. It just fucking ruined all of my plans.*

Me: *Safety first. That's what matters, right?*

Malik: *I guess (:*

He sent a photo.

It was a photo of him laying in bed with his head propped up on a blue pillow. It felt as though he were staring right into my eyes, even though I knew that the only way he could do that would be through a video call. I was too stunned by his good looks to remember that he awaited a response from me. Once I snapped out of my trance, however, I sent him the first words that made it to my lips.

Me: *You look good.*

Malik: *Thank you.*

Malik: *Hey, do you mind sending a photo as well?*

My eyes remained fixed on my screen, reading Malik's message for what could have been a million times in only a few minutes. When he sent a photo, I had known to expect that he would want me to send him a live photo as well, yet his request unsettled me anyway. He must have realized from my delayed response that his request had tossed my mood into disarray.

Malik: *Heeeey, it's okay, I get it.*

Malik: *you don't have to send a pic if you aren't comfortable with it*

When I received his most recent message, I was already trying to take a selfie. I straightened my spine and stared into my camera with what I thought would be an absolutely fake smile. But once the photo clicked, I realized that the smile was the realest I had generated in a long time. If it wasn't for the chubbiness of my cheeks and the noticeably wide flare of my nostrils, I would consider myself a pretty brunette. I'd been trying not to dwell on the extra pounds that just wouldn't go away, but Anderson's thoughtlessness was making this a much harder fight.

I sent the photo to Malik, and with bated breath, I awaited his response. Barely a moment after I sent the photo, Malik started to type.

And then his message popped up: *OMG!*

Malik: *Damn! You are so sexy!*

Sexy? That's new, I thought with a smile.

Thank you. That was my response to him. My cheeks heated up as I read his words all over again.

Malik: *Well, Ashley, I'll say this once again. Only a blind man would consider you fat.*

Me: *Well, fat is all he sees when he looks at me.*

By 'he', Malik knew I was referring to my husband. My post to the BDD support group was a photo of me wearing the controversial black dress and a telling of the story behind it. I'd written about how I'd added extra weight after childbirth and how my husband no longer found me pleasing to his senses, so Malik knew that the woman he was currently chatting with was a mother and a wife.

He sent a new message: *You have no idea the things I'd do to you if I was the one so close to you.*

I replied: *What would you do to me?*

He sent a wink emoji.

And then another message: *you don't wanna know.*

Me: *Try me.*

Malik*: I'd treat you right, Ash. In and outta bed.*

Malik: *I'd worship you like the queen that you are.*

Malik: *Eat your pussy until you squirt all over my face.*

When he spoke about doings things to me, I'd known right away that those words could only mean naughty things. Despite the ring on my finger, I smiled with intrigue and my pussy pulsated with need.

Malik: *I wanna do dirty things to you, Ash.*

Malik: *But only if you let me.*

Malik: *Will you?*

Me: *If you promise to be gentle.*

I sent a kissy face and he returned my kiss almost immediately.

Malik: *Oh Ash. I promise. I will give you no cause for complaint. None at all. Only a pleasure fitting for a queen.*

Malik: *I'd ask what color of panties you are wearing at the moment but I won't.*

Me: *Why?*

Malik: *Because I want to find out for myself when I part your legs, my queen. I will slowly part your legs to reveal your pantie. I know that it is already soaked with your juices.*

I glanced down at my thighs, and detached my left hand from my phone to feel the state of my underwear. My pantie was soaked, just as Malik had guessed.

Malik: *I know that you're touching yourself now, wanting to feel your own wetness. Don't stop at just feeling it, Ash.*

I sucked in a deep breath and my panty-clad pussy throbbed against my fingers. While my left hand stayed glued to my underwear, pressing the gusset into my throbbing flesh, my other hand singlehandedly typed a response to Malik.

What will you have me do, Malik? I sent the message to him and relaxed my left hand against my pussy as I awaited his response.

Malik: *touch yourself, Ash.*

Malik: *I want you to touch yourself.*

I gulped heavily and mentally prepared myself to follow the man's command. I didn't know this man at all, yet I found that I was beginning to trust him enough to entertain no doubt that he would bring me the all pleasure I craved. I expanded the waistband of my pantie and attempted to glide my fingers down the bare skin leading to my juiciness, but his next message caused me to halt.

Malik: *I want you to tease yourself through your pantie.*

Me: *Why?*

Malik: *Because I want every inch of your gusset to be soaked with your juices. And I would like a photo of your soaked pantie, just so I can tell you're being a good girl.*

Me: *What do I get if I'm a good girl?*

Malik: A photo of my eight inch dick, Ashley. Hard and ready, waiting to glide into your buttery smooth pussy and worship you inside out.

Oh God. I wanted this man so badly inside of me. An eight inch cock was a few centimeters longer than my husband's. I wondered if it was just as thicker as it was longer. I'd never thought I would ever let a stranger gratify himself with the arousing sight of my wet pantie. But at that moment, I would do anything just to see the eight inch goodness that was all hard and ready for me.

So, I did just as Malik had ordered. I fingered myself through my pantie.

Two
Jason Scooper

I set down a cup of coffee on my husband's work desk. The man was too swamped with work to even tear his eyes away from his monitor as he picked up the cup.

"Careful," I said. "It's hot."

"Thank you," he said.

Thank you? Really? That was the best he could do? He didn't even have a moment to look up into my eyes as he expressed gratitude. I had known not to expect a worthy response form Matthias, yet my heart clenched disappointedly. Without another word, I vacated the study and walked down the corridor leading to our bedroom.

As though my phone had been waiting for me the whole time I was away, it beeped, demanding my full attention. I walked over to the phone and my eyes briefly caught my reflection in the mirrored closet as I walked past. My reflection only held my attention for the split of a second, and then I picked up my phone.

I had just received a new message from an unfamiliar man.

It better be good. I was sick of scammers flooding my inbox with dumb schemes that only a fool would fall for. I clicked on the chat head to view the stranger's message.

"What the fuck?" I glanced behind to ensure that Matthias was nowhere in sight. My blood heated with rage as I returned my attention to the phone and the image on the screen.

The nerves of that man! How dare he even send a photo of his cock? How shameless could a human possibly be? At first thought, confronting the jerk seemed like a perfect idea. But I would not give him the attention he sought, so I unfriended him right away.

Jason Scooper.

His name didn't ring a bell. And I'd always thought that everyone on my Facebook friend's list were people I knew in person. At some point when I was younger, I'd received unsolicited sexually explicit images in my inbox on a daily basis. That was the sole reason I'd unfriended every stranger, cutting down my friend's list from two thousand to three hundred. Jason Scooper must have escaped unnoticed.

I wanted to believe that unfriending the stranger would be enough to erase the memory of his cock. But who was I kidding? The image was stuck in my memory, the same way a gothic rose tattoo had been stuck to my left shoulder since I was eighteen.

Leading my thoughts away from the man's endowment was an overpowering struggle I faced until bedtime, when my husband lay on his side of our bed. I reached out to touch him, but my hand froze in mid-air, barely even an inch away from his body.

Maybe he needed to rest.

For some reason best known to him, he had been overworking himself lately. Now that he was finally in bed, I would have to leave him to rest, even though it had been painfully long since he last made love to me.

Sleep would come easy if I wasn't so troubled. Hours ago when I unfriended the stranger who had sent me an image of his cock, I had been convinced that I'd made the right decision. I mean, who randomly sends nudes to strangers?

Well, a stupid man could. And a bold man could as well. And then there was a different kind of man—one who was neither stupid nor bold, but was a crazy mix of both. My phone beeped with a notification and I grabbed it right away.

'Jason Scooper sent you a friend request.'

My pussy tingled at once I saw his name, and my whole body burned with desire in a way it should never respond to a man who wasn't my husband. While it would be unfair to Matthias to give myself to another man while we remained legally married, it would be unfair to myself to let my desires remain unsatiated for so long.

Jason's chat head popped up on my screen with the usual ringing of the Messenger notification bell.

"Damn it woman!" Matthias groaned. "I'm trying to get some sleep."

He buried his face in his pillow and held the position for a few unsettling minutes.

"Sorry..." I turned on my 'do not disturb' mode.

But was I really sorry?

At the moment, the only thing I cared about was a means to gratify my sexual urges which had been left unattended for an outrageously long time. If Matthias insisted on choosing his job over my needs, then I was totally in for whatever the daring stranger had to offer. I returned my attention to my phone screen, and before I could read the new massage Jason had just sent, his huge cock caught my eye once again. This time, I made no attempt to resist the emotions surging inside of me. Warmth flooded my insides and my senses seemed to heighten as I stared at the glorious sight on my screen. Thick veins stretched along his cock, making me want to trace them with my tongue and make him glossy with my spit.

I read his message: *Something is missing.*

I grimaced. Missing? What could actually be missing? Was that why he'd added me back? To tell me that something was missing?

I received another message from him: *right?*

I sent a reply: *I don't understand.*

Jason: *my cock.*

Jason: *look at it.*

Jason: *closely.*

Jason: *see it now?*

His messages were coming in so fast I barely had time to read each one before proceeding to the next. The photo of his cock leapt up, out of eyeshot, demanding that I scroll up to see it once again. I scrolled up to meet the picture, and my breath caught in my throat as though I were staring at the impressive sight for the very first time.

I could only see how huge he was between his legs. I had no idea what he thought was missing. He had all a man could ever wish to have.

I scrolled back down to see a new message from him.

Jason: *seen it?*

Me: *What exactly am I looking for?*

Jason: *whatever is missing in the picture.*

He sent a wink emoji, and then a cucumber.

Me: *You should just tell me already.*

Jason: *cum.*

I was quiet for a moment, allowing his word sink in. But in no time, I gave up on trying to understand him on my own.

Me: *That's what's missing?*

Jason: *yh*

Jason: *i was hoping you could help me complete the picture. you know...*

Me: *How do I do that?*

Jason: *make me cum.*

Me: *Oh...*

I could understand that he wanted me to chat dirty with him. It seemed to be the only way I could make him come, considering that we were so far away from each other. He would be appalled to learn that I sucked at dirty chatting.

So I let him know right away: *I suck at sex chatting.*

He sent a happy face emoji.

Then a message: *you're putting too much pressure on yourself.*

And then another: *just don't do that.*

And yet another: *know what? just follow my lead. for a start, tell me what you're wearing.*

I replied: *My night dress*

Jason: *yummy*

Jason: *panties?*

Me: *yeah*

He sent a heart-eyes emoji.

Jason: *so sexy, babe. i wanna peel that dress off your sexy body. inch by inch. slowly slipping the straps down your arms and kissing you as i uncover each inch of your body.*

My breath started to thin out, and soon, it was barely even enough to fill my lungs. It felt like Jason's arms were all over me, slowly stripping off my dress just as he'd said he would.

Jason: *i want to cover every inch of your neck with kisses while i wrap my arms around you from behind and slowly glide my hands up your sexy body until I have your breasts caged in my firm grip. your nipples are so hard...so perky...suckable...*

Me: *What keeps you from sucking them already?*

Jason: *i want to take my time with you, darling. a work of art must be approached cautiously. that is why I must take my time with you. my cock is so damn hard...*

Jason: *wait...*

He sent another photo of his cock.

"Oh my gosh!" I muttered, as though he were here to hear me.

The glorious sight of his cock had suddenly made me oblivious to everything else; even to Matthias' presence. It was only after those words left my lips that I remembered Matthias was in bed with me. I looked up at him and was pleased to find that he was sound asleep—if his immobile state was any indication of that.

Making a mental note to be totally silent this time, I looked back at Jason's cock. When he sent me the first photo a few hours ago, I had thought that was the hardest he could get. Now though, I realized just how wrong I had been. He was noticeably a few centimeters longer than he had been the other time. My pussy throbbed and clenched, preparing itself for a hard thrust as though there was a way to bring Jason home to me.

I sent a message to him: *Wow! You are so hard.*

He replied: *fully erect. just for you.*

I pressed my thighs into each other, giving my pussy a subtle stimulation in an attempt to dull the she starting to build up between my legs.

Jason: *mmmm. while I embrace you from behind, I want to lean into you and press my erection into you, gliding it in-between your ass without letting go of your soft breasts.*

Jason: *would you like that?*

Me: *I'd like it better if you started to knead my ass crack with your cock.*

Jason: *you are not afraid of my girth, are you?*

Me: *I like my men huge.*

Jason: *now you're daring me, woman.*

Me: *Fuck me, Jason. I want you to. I want to feel you deep inside of me. I want to know what it feels like to take in a rod as huge as yours. Please...*

Jason: *go on. tell me the things you want me to do to you.*

I want you to... Once I started to type, Jason started to type as well.

Jason: *no no.*

Jason: *don't type.*

Jason: *i wanna hear you say those words. i wanna hear the filthiness in your voice as you beg me to fuck you.*

Jason: *send a vn.*

Jason: *now.*

Jason was feeling bolder now, ordering me around as though he were my master. I could say no to him, for the sake of my dignity. But I did the exact opposite.

As stealthily as I could, I vacated the bed and strode to the bathroom. Closing the door behind me, I walked into the shower compartment. I trusted that the opaque walls of the shower compartment would not give my voice a chance to drift outside the bathroom.

I cleared my throat, and then I tapped and held the microphone icon on my screen. "I want you to fuck me, Jason. I want you to pin me down on your bed and hold my heads apart to grant you access to my tight pussy. It's so warm and wet, slippery enough for you to glide through. I'm in my bathroom right now, still clad in my night dress."

I slipped my left hand beneath my dress and moved my gusset aside. Once it was out of the way, I glided my index finger inside of me and a moan escaped my lips. My finger inched deeper, burrowing a narrow hole and eliciting more moans of pleasure.

I released the icon and sent the voice recording. He was mute for a minute or two, and I worried that I had done something wrong. After another minute of awaiting a response, he finally sent a new message.

It was a three-seconds video of a short burst of cum erupting from his meatus

and traveling down his shaft.

Three

Hot for Two

Valentine would be great.

Frederick and I had always wanted a romantic moment together, so the lockdown would give us all the time we needed to spend the 14th of February in each other's arms. Needing to spice things up, I had ordered a sexy lingerie set from an online store. Frederick was an 'ass man'—if that made any sense. My ass was the first thing he'd noticed about me when we first met, and after four years together, it remained an asset he never got tired of groping. So I had made sure to get a garter set that would not conceal my ass from his sultry eyes. The lingerie held a shade of red similar to the color of the rose tattoo on my left rib cage, and yet it paired perfectly with the golden yellow of my wavy hair.

Checking out my reflection in my mirror one last time, I tiptoed out of my walk-in closet. Frederick had known me for vanilla sex since the start of our relationship, and now I decided it was time to step out of my comfort zone and step up our love life. He apparently wasn't set to make the first move, so I had taken it upon myself to do it.

February 14th was a Sunday. Thank heavens!

Since the lockdown, my husband had suddenly transformed into a workaholic—something he had never been known for. He literally spent all day at his desk, working until his bones ached. He didn't have a choice though. He worked as a customer care representative at a high-end digital bank and was one of the few who had not been laid off to cut down on organizational expenses during the pandemic. A drastic reduction in the number of employees meant an overworking of the few employees the organization had left. And, recently, there had been an overwhelming number of clients queuing up to speak with a customer care representative, making it almost impossible for Frederick to even remember to have lunch or empty his bladder whenever the need arose.

He didn't work on Saturdays and Sundays though. Those were the only days I could have him all to myself. It made me look over to weekends the like a student fed up with having to wake up at six on weekday mornings to prepare for school. It would be great to walk up to him from behind without making a sound, and then make known my presence with my fingers gliding down his torso or giving his shoulders a brief massage. But my feet were enclosed in killer heels that that could never meet the tiled floor without a loud click announcing my presence. I could discard the shoes and choose to walk on my bare feet instead, but my outfit would be incomplete without the heels. Well, mostly because I needed some luxury footwear to complement my thigh-high stockings.

My heels were loud against the floor as I stepped out of the closet. I didn't have to look around for Frederick. He was right there, at his work desk. He, however, wasn't swamped with work this time. Instead, he was engrossed in the a game he enjoyed so much—PUBG. He sat there in front of his monitor, with his headphones plugged into his ears.

I sighed. Whenever it was time to game, racking up kills was the only thing that mattered to him. I could consider my purpose already defeated, but I remembered seeing some TikTok videos where ladies approached their men in sheer nudity, and seven times out of ten, the men would ditch their games for some quality time.

It had been unbearably long without some quality time with Frederick. I knew deep down, that he wanted me just as much as I wanted him. If it wasn't for the cursed pandemic and the nationwide lockdown it had brought upon us, Frederick and I would be away from home to celebrate Valentine's day at some fancy place, the same way we did each year. As engrossed as he was in his game, however, I trusted that my curvaceous body would pull him to me like a magnetized piece of metal.

I took a step, and then another in his direction. But he kept playing his game. I could only imagine the thunderous noise spilling out of his headphones. I crossed the room to meet him, and when I halted behind him, I placed my palms on both sides of his chest and glided them down toward the waistband of his pants.

"No no." He shrugged, as though to rid himself of me. "I'm heading for an air drop. Can't afford to get distracted right now."

I played deaf to his words and kept my palms gliding down until my fingers brushed his cock through his pants. I was leaning forward now, my chest resting on his body.

"Megan!" He rose to his feet and tossed his console to his desk. "Good grief! I just fucking got sniped!"

He looked up at me and then he froze. Literally. His eyes roamed my body, from my chest to my feet, and back up into my eyes.

"Damn, babe!" He ran his fingers through his hair, and then he stepped forward with a smile. "You look so fucking hot."

I returned his smile. I had been right to think that there was no way he could possibly choose a video game over all of this sexiness.

"All for you," I said, my voice barely even a whisper.

He wrapped his arms around me and yanked me close. The motion rendered me breathless, and just when I tried to refill my lungs, he kissed me hard on the lips. He led me backward, into a wall and peppered down kisses from my lips to my neck and shoulders. I tilted my head sideways, baring my neck to him. I let my eyelids fall over my eyes, shutting out every sight. With my eyes so tightly shut, I stared into a thick darkness interrupted by splatters of colors.

"I've missed you so much baby!" I said.

"And I you, my darling."

His voice was loud and clear, but it wasn't the only voice I could hear. I had totally forgotten about his headphone, but once I remembered that the device was stealing away his attention, I opened my eyes and moved to yank it off his head. I had been craving my man's full attention for so long, and now that I finally had him right where I wanted him, I had no intentions of sharing.

But Frederick did not let me get on with what I was about to do. He had been kissing me with his eyes wide open, and once he saw me attempt to yank off his headphones, he stepped backward and repositioned the device on his head.

"One sec, bro!" he said. Not to me. But to his teammates on the other end of the device.

He stared apologetically into my eyes, and then he leaned forward to plant a brief kiss on my lips.

"I'm sorry," he said. "But my guys are inviting for another match."

"Don't..." I grabbed his left arm to stop him.

He did stop, but the look in his eyes told me not to get my hopes up.

"Only for a moment," he said. "Then I'm all yours..."

"Bro?" a voice rang out from his headphone.

Frederick stared into my eyes. I hoped that he could see right through me, and read me like an open book. I hoped he could see just how badly my heart was breaking with the thought that he was about to leave me for some dumb game he'd been playing his whole life as though he earned a thousand dollars for every win. I hoped that the tears glistening in my eyes would be enough to make him stay.

I desperately wanted to believe that Frederick wouldn't be so insensitive as to ignore my hurt.

But he did turn away.

He slipped his hand out of my grip, and then he was gone, back at his desk to play another dumb match. I stood there frozen in time, my legs suddenly feeling too heavy to be lifted off the ground. The tears in my eyes finally found a way out. They streaked down my cheeks, creating wet trails to evidence my pain.

While I stood frozen, I kept my eyes fixated on the spot there Frederick had been standing in front of me. I could not bring myself to look in his direction as he returned to his game. I wanted to detach myself from reality and feign oblivion to his game, but when I heard him apologizing to his teammates for taking so long, my heart heaved painfully. It wasn't enough that he'd turned me down after I'd tried so hard to please his senses. Here he was now, apologizing to his teammates as though I didn't matter to him the way they did.

When I finally brought myself to look at him, I clenched my jaw with a resolve to avenge myself. I swiped across my cheeks with my finger pads and then I headed for our bed where my phone lay beneath a pillow. I lay down in bed and grabbed the phone.

If Frederick would give me no attention, then it was his loss and not mine. There were men vying for my attention. But I'd ignored them all, just so I would not be distracted from fully pleasing my husband—a man who had just showed me that he deserved no such loyalty.

I took a photo of myself with a focus on my breasts, and with a hopeful smile, I sent it to Kennedy—an ex I was still friends with. Kennedy did not care that there was another man in my life. He still wanted me in bed with him anyway, and now, for the first time, I was considering his proposal to let him in as the 'other man' in my life.

Kennedy sent a message just as soon as he saw my photo.

Kennedy: *Jesus fucking Christ!*

Kennedy: *You're so fucking hot, mami.*

Me: *Thank you. (:*

Kennedy: *Such a shame you won't let me treat you right.*

Me: *Such a shame you're giving up so soon, Ken.*

Kennedy: *Wait...what?*

He sent a laughing emoji.

Kennedy: *You're not trying to fuck with me, are you?*

Me: *Depends on the type of fucking you're referring to. If you're talking about me playing games with you, then no, I'm not. But if you're speaking of a penile-vaginal penetration, then yes, Kennedy. I'll totally fuck with you.*

Kennedy: *Penile-vaginal? Why so formal?*

I laughed out loud.

And then I replied: *I have no idea.*

Kennedy: *I want to fuck you, mami. The pic you sent...Good heavens! It has made me so fucking hard...*

Kennedy: *Wanna see?*

Me: *Yes, please.*

He sent a photo of his cock. Well, of the bulge in his pants. It was a little disappointing to see his pants keeping his cock out of sight, but my disappointment melted away when I dwelled on the fact that I had made a virile man so hard without even trying. His cock was almost bursting through his pants.

Kennedy: *He's hard and veiny. Just the way you like it.*

Images of his cock darted through my mind's eye. I could vividly remember him pinning me to his bed while he glided his thick cock inside of me, hammering me so hard we disturbed the serenity of his neighborhood with our animalistic screams.

A new message from Kennedy cut through my thoughts.

Kennedy: *He wants to glide inside of you, babe. Tear you apart the way he used to.*

My pussy ached with need as it craved the thickness of Kennedy's cock. It was a sensation I could not feign oblivion to. It started out as a dull ache, and then it intensified, spreading through my body and causing me to tremble with an insatiable craving for something out of reach. I parted my legs, slid my fingers beneath the waistband of my pantie and all the way down until I felt the slimy wetness of my pussy.

And then I thrust.

My pussy spread apart to accommodate my fingers, and my lips spread simultaneously, letting out a moan. I closed my eyes as a slowly intensifying pleasure built up between my legs. And just before I closed my eyes, I saw a totally unclad Frederick advancing toward me.

Four

Home Alone

I had never been one for new friends.

Especially not on Facebook with people I'd never met before.

But when Kyle and I chatted for the very first time, everything just fell into place, as though he were a part of my past life. I must say though, that chatting with him made me feel older in a way I had never felt before. Not in a bad way though. He considered me a MILF, even though I personally didn't think thirty-two was old enough to be considered a MILF. I didn't blame him though. He would be twenty-two in a few weeks, and according to him, I reminded him of his biology teacher—one Mrs. Adams he had always dreamed of fucking.

Kyle had an adventurous spirit I just couldn't get enough of. That was undoubtedly one of the things that attracted me to him so badly. That and the fact that he reminded me of my first boyfriend, Aiden.

Aiden was blond haired, just like Kyle, and was also on the tall side, with an athletic body that many men dreamed of having. I didn't mean to compare Kyle with my first boyfriend, but their many similarities were impossible to ignore. It made me wonder if Kyle was as huge between his legs as Aiden was. Aiden's endowment was one I couldn't forget in a hurry. He'd been my first, and as though that wasn't enough to make him unforgettable, he'd fucked me in a way no other man ever had, with a vigor that always made me hopelessly sore when he was done. I'd been married to my interracial man, Sebastian, for two years, and although he fucked me almost every night, it was never enough for me to get over Aiden. So, when he went for his usual appointment with his ophthalmologist, I knew this was a heaven-made moment for me to have my own slice of lockdown fun.

I texted Kyle right away: *Guess who's home alone?*

A winking emoji accompanied my question.

Kyle: *OMG! For reals?*

Me: *Yh, hubby just went for an appointment with his eye doctor.*

I awaited a reply from Kyle, and after minutes of waiting, what I got was a call on Messanger instead. We had ben texting for five days, and this was the first time I would ever get to hear his voice. My chest fluttered with nervous anticipation as I answered the phone.

"How long will he be away?" Kyle asked. His voice was deep and absolutely sexy, complimenting his good looks.

"I'd say an hour at most," I said.

I was standing beside one of the two windows in my living room. I looked through the window and scanned the desolate streets even though I knew that my husband was already far gone. He'd left no less than ten minutes ago, and the road was as free as never before. The man always drove at breakneck speed as though he had been a racer at some point in his life, so I knew he was only a few minutes away from arriving at the eye clinic.

"I'm coming over," Kyle said.

I found his boldness alarming, and for a brief moment, all I did was muse over his words. He hadn't asked for permission to come over. He had only informed me that he would come over. He was only so bold because I let him. If I hadn't chatted dirty with him three nights in a row, he wouldn't be bold enough to want to come to my place. I found it just as thrilling as it was alarming, and could not feign oblivion to the sudden contraction of my pussy as it craved a cock.

"How do you intend to bypass the security?" I asked, genuinely concerned.

The words had barely even made it through my lips when I heard the wailing of sirens. I glanced through the window and watched a series of police cruisers roam the streets.

"Do you hear that?" I asked.

"Nothing to worry about," he said.

This was the fourth lockdown since the start of the pandemic. Now more than ever, the cops were stricter with enforcing lockdown rules and would show no mercy to anyone who had no valid reasons to not stay at home. They could fine him, use reasonable force, or worse, charge him with a criminal offense. Yet, Kyle didn't even seem one bit bothered.

"I need your address," he said.

"I'm still wondering how you're gonna get through the cops."

"I have my ways."

***

Truly, he did have his ways.

Only a few minutes after I dropped my phone, I heard the doorbell. I bolted to the door and yanked it open. I had known from Kyle's pictures that he was on the tall side, but I just hadn't thought I would have to tilt my head up to gaze into his eyes. He regarded me with a soft smile, and then his gaze flicked to my chest, taking in the juicy sight of my full breasts. I had showered just after our phone call ended, and then I'd clad myself in sexy thigh-high stockings and a garter belt.

I was all black. Well, save for my red hair and my porcelain skin.

"You look so sexy." He wrapped his left arm around me and yanked so hard I fell against his chest.

In this position, I could feel his heartbeat pulsing through his shirt. As hyperactive as his heart was, it did not come close to mine. My heart was beating so fast it brought a tremor to my whole body.

Remembering the compliment I'd left hanging in the air, I smiled at him. "Thank you. So do you."

"You'll look even better…" He winked at me. "With my cock inside of you."

He smiled back at me and squeezed the left globe of my ass.

"When I saw your pic for the first time…" He led me backward, toward a couch. He was staring down into my face the whole time, his hard cock poking me through his pants. "…all I wanted was to fuck you…"

He flicked a lock of hair away from my face, and when he tucked it behind my left ear, he simultaneously leaned in for a kiss. His lips were firm and demanding, knocking me out of breath the moment they met mine. Desperate to refill my lungs with oxygen, I tilted my head back, but his lips were stuck on mine as though there was an invisible glue binding us together. When his lips finally left mine, he kissed his way down to my neck and centered on the almost unnoticeable bulge of my Adam's apple. My frantic hands started to roam his body. Upon finding the hem of his top, I slowly pulled it up toward his head. Once I rid him of the fabric, he placed a firm hand on my shoulder and guided me to the floor. My knees met the floor and I straightened my spine, positioning my head just in front of the bulge in his pants as I watched him unbelt. While I feasted my eyes on the intriguing sight of his pants giving way, I moved my hair away from my face and to the back of my head, where they would not dare interfere in my pleasure.

Kyle's pants dropped down his body and his underpants followed suit, revealing the thick rod I had been dying to see. I gasped at the sight of it, and he cupped my face to stare into my eyes.

"Do you like?" he asked.

I nodded, and then I licked my lips. He was yet to connect with my mouth and yet I could already taste him on my lips. He was just as huge as I had imagined. Probably even huger than the ex whose memory was stuck in my head. And I was just about to find out just how good he was with his endowment.

He grabbed my head and pushed it forward, causing me to fall face-first against his crotch. His cock tore my lips apart and slipped right between the warm walls of my mouth. I moaned in acceptance of the pleasure already rippling through me. Kyle added a firm pressure to his grip, and just as my lips glided down toward the base of his cock, he simultaneously thrust forward, nailing my throat with his hard rod. I gasped, taken aback by his suddenness, but his tight grip on my head gave me no chance to move away. He held me in place, forcing me to hold his cock in my throat.

Kyle was almost balls-deep inside of me, so I'd thought he'd go no further. But then he suddenly shoved his cock deeper, slamming it into my tonsils. My stomach clenched in a preparation to empty its contents as the gag reflex suddenly stole me over. Gagging on Kyles' cock was not enough reason to get him to pull away though. Spit gathered in my mouth and started to dribble down both corners.

With Kyle so deep inside of me, it was impossible to breathe. I tried to breathe through my nose, but it was just as pointless as trying to sniff with a pinched nose. After moments of Kyle blocking my airways, he eased his way out of my throat and started to fuck my face with relatively shallow thrusts. My head bobbed back and forth, my hair flying all over my face as he picked up pace. His breathing was loud and labored, but it was not enough to drown out the sloshing and gaging sounds he generated as he pounded his way toward my throat once again.

And then, suddenly, he held still.

But he didn't slacken his hold on my head. His cock twitched inside of me, and then I felt a familiar warmth filling my mouth. He yanked me to my feet and crushed his lips into mine, lapping up some of the hot spunk he had just deposited in my mouth.

I had never seen—or heard of—a man eating his own cum. But he did not give me a moment to dwell on this irregularity. He plopped down on the couch nearest to us and pulled me onto his laps so I straddled him with my back to him. My pussy tingled in anticipation of his hard cock, so I gyrated my ass around him, teasing him with the sliminess he would soon explore.

Kyle had another plan though—one I didn't know of until he grabbed my legs and suspended them in the air to reveal my tight ass which had been left unattended to since the start of my relationship with Sebastian. I froze at the feel of his fat tip at my entrance. My heart thumped in my chest as I gave in to a genuine fear evoked by the size of his cock.

"Kyle..." I whispered in a breathy voice.

"Shhh." He kissed my neck and shoulders, and then he sucked hard on my left shoulder.

I didn't realize his intention was to give me a hickey until it was all too late to stop him. His lips clamped down so hard on my skin that it would be impossible for me to pry then off. He added a firm pressure to his cock and thrashed his way through my sphincter. My ass clenched defensively, but it only spurred him to double the pressure with which he penetrated my tightness.

He thrust a little harder than my tight ass could take calmly, and I winced. A cry tore my lips apart as I sought to break free, but Kyle held me in a vice-like grip, pinning me down on his cock and forcing me to take in his full length.

Once he was fully inside of me, he started to thrust. But we came to a standstill when we heard the jiggle of keys behind the door.

Sebastian.

Five

An Almost Threesome

'I miss you so much, my love.'

It didn't matter that Jeremy and I had been married for eleven, words like these always evoked emotions similar to the emotions a confession of love would evoke in a teenage girl. My fingers raced across my keypad, and in barely even two seconds, I typed a fitting response to his text.

'I miss you too, my darling.'

Jeremy replied almost immediately.

Jeremy: *How much do you miss me?*

Me: *More than you know.*

I had never missed anyone so intensely. It felt as though a part of me had been detached from my body, leaving behind an overwhelming emptiness.

Jeremy was far away in Italy on a business trip. He'd been sent to supervise the construction of the Italian branch of the telecommunications company where he worked, and had been scheduled to return home to Los Angeles in the next three months.

Three months without each other had seemed like forever, and we had both been counting down to seeing each other again. Little did we know that a virus made in China would plunge the whole world into darkness. It had been week after week of lockdown in Italy as well as in the United States, with the rate of new infections steadily increasing. We both knew that there was absolutely no hope of us seeing each other anytime soon—not until our countries eased the temporary ban on all flights. Left without a choice, Jeremy and I had long accepted that we could only spend time through calling and texting.

Just when my phone screen started to dim, Jeremy dropped a new message in my inbox.

Jeremy: *what are you doing?*

Me: *texting you. Lol.*

Jeremy: *no, hun. I mean what are you doing for reals???*

Me: *oh, just laying down. How about you?*

Jeremy: *stroking my cock.*

I gasped. I most definitely hadn't seen that coming. I had expected a response as casual and innocent as mine, so I had not been prepared for the sudden clenching of my pussy that preceded his message.

Jeremy: *wanna c?*

I laughed. Since when did Jeremy start needing permission? It didn't matter if I said yes or no or didn't reply at all, he would still go on ahead to do his thing. If I knew him well enough—and I sure did—then I'd say that he was already capturing a detailed picture of his eight inch endowment. As expected, he sent me a photo of his cock right away. He was laying in bed, with his pants riding low on his waist to let out his cock. His cock was just as thick as I remembered, with a fat tip that always knocked me out of breath each time he made his way inside of me. Although his cock was just as I remembered, I desired it in a way I never had before.

Jeremy sent a message. *you miss it, don't you?*

Me: *I'd be lying to say otherwise.*

Jeremy: *then come get it, darling.*

Me: *Haha. I wish.*

A video call came in right away, stretching my lips toward my ears. I was in a rather awkward position when the call came in, so I took a moment to adjust myself. I straightened my spine and aligned my back with the backrest of my bed, and then I answered the call. Jeremy was in the same position as I. The only difference was that he was totally shirtless while I was wearing a silky red night robe. He smiled at the sight of me, and then a gleam crept into his eyes once his gaze flicked down to my chest.

"Beautiful,"" he said. "You look even sexier, my love. You're all aglow with joy."

I looked away with a sheepish smile. I feared that if I held his gaze for much longer, he would be able to see through my eyes and know that I was hiding something from him.

"...as though you had a reason to be so joyous," he said pensively.

I looked up at him. "You, Jeremy. I'm happy to have you."

"Same here, my love." He kissed me through the phone. "I hear that distance only makes the heart grow fonder. Well, I think some other organ—"

He made quotation marks with his free hand.

"--is growing fonder too." He lowered his phone and aimed his camera at his groin, flooding my vision with his enormous cock.

"I wish you were here..." I sighed.

"Yeah..." While he held his phone with his right hand, he brought his left hand to his cock and slowly glided his fingers along his shaft. "If we were together I wouldn't be touching myself..."

He looked up into my eyes with a smile, and then he held my gaze, making sure he had my full attention. My eyes were fixated on him, watching his every move. That was enough proof that he held my full attention.

Or so I wanted him to believe.

Jeremy would never know that he only held half of my attention. He would never know that there was another man in bed with me, creeping between my legs and parting them even more to accommodate his body. There were times when my cravings went over the rooftop. This was one of those times. After an unbearably long period of celibacy, I finally realized that my husband's absence wasn't enough to make me abstain from sex. I'd gotten myself a hitachi wand and a big black dildo, and while they were great at driving me to orgasm, they didn't give me the absolute sexual gratification I craved.

But Harry did.

He was a next door neighbor--a widower I'd always considered sexy but had no idea of his filthiness until my husband's absence. My pussy could already feel his presence. It clenched with need, welcoming a ripple of pleasure as Harry brushed a tentative finger along its soft warm folds. He trailed his fingers along my inner thighs, alleviating my desire for the hardness between his legs. It didn't matter that he had fucked me into a pulp barely an hour ago; I needed him all over again, working me to orgasm while I watched Jeremy jerk off to my moans. Could that be considered a threesome?

"Oh God!" I gasped and winced.

I hadn't thought that Harry was with my hitachi want until I felt an intense vibration on my clitoral hood.

"Are you okay?" Jeremy asked, his eyes staring a deep hole through me.

I parted my lips and tried to speak, but the intensifying vibrations of the wand flushed my words down my throat and had me moaning instead. My whole body stiffened with pleasure and the balls of my feet dug into the bed, reaching deeper until they couldn't go any further.

I could tell Jeremy that I was alright. But my husband was no fool. I knew that being a drama queen was the only way to redeem myself. So, I cupped my lips with my free hand and sobbed into my palm.

"I miss you..." I cried. "So so bad. I just can't stand this anymore. Each moment you're not here...it feels..."

I gasped. *Oh my gosh!*

I had just felt a velvety warm organ gliding along my pussy. I could tell, without looking down at Harry, that he had just introduced his tongue. Yet, I glanced down at him anyway, catching a look in his eyes that instantly tossed my insides into disarray.

"...this long distance is killing me, my love," I cried.

The vibrator buzzed against my clitoral hood, and in no time, the sound grew louder. I cocked an eye at Jeremy and tried to figure out whether he could hear the sound. If he could, he made no attempt to show it.

"Touch yourself," he said.

"No," I protested. "I would rather wait until you're here..."

"Listen to me, Amber!" he said.

My pussy tightened around Harry's fingers as they suddenly glided between my throbbing walls. I nodded, a little too vigorous for normalcy. This was me trying to contain my pleasure as Harry curled up his fingers inside of me and started to hit my G-spot. But Jeremy apparently though this was me pledging my undivided attention to him. My throat throbbed with a scream, but I masqueraded the sound as a frustrated cry instead.

I shook my head. "It won't feel good, my love. Not as good as you inside of me."

A few moments ago, Jeremy had tilted his camera away from his cock so I could see his face as he spoke to me. Now though, he aimed the camera at his cock once again, flooding my vision with the sight of him stroking himself.

"You know I'm dying to be inside you." He ran his fingers along his shaft, all the way down, and then back up toward his tip.

His heartbeat accelerated noticeably, matching mine as Harry kept pumping me with his fingers.

"I want to watch you fuck yourself, Amber," he said.

I glanced down at Harry, and into his sultry eyes as though I needed his permission before responding to my husband's request. He nodded at me just before he drove his tongue deep inside of me. I cried out and rocked my head back, my legs visibly trembling when he started to flick his tongue around my tightness. When he flicked his tongue around like that, it was impossible to keep still.

I trembled and cried out, my heart beating heavily. My chest heaved with each breath and I grabbed his head in an attempt to lessen the intensity of his tongue action.

"Oh fuck!" Jeremy cried. "That's it baby! Cry for me! Louder!"

My phone trembled in my grip and threatened to slither away, and when my palm turned clammy, holding on to my phone seemed impossible.

"I can't--" I cried out.

"Don't stop baby!" Jeremy picked up steam, his hands moving at a pace that would drive him to orgasm in no time. He moaned into the phone, his voice loud and raspy as it thrashed its way through my eardrums.

Harry pulled away from my pussy and set down the hitachi wand on the bed. And, just when I thought he would give me the luxury of a breather, he raised himself to his knees and his hard cock aimed right at my slippery hole. My pussy throbbed in anticipation of his hardness, to feel him skin to skin, grinding into me with an intensity that would make the bed tremble beneath us. He grabbed my legs, spread them apart, and without warning, yanked me down toward his cock, instantly impaling me. I cried out and wiggled, and at that moment, my grip on my phone slackened enough to let it slither away.

I made no attempt to pick up my fallen phone. I let it lay there, shutting out the sight of me so Jeremy could only hear my screams of pleasure. Harry's grip tightening on my legs, he thrust deeper inside of me.

His cock was so huge, eliciting a scream as he went balls-deep inside of me. Harry filled me completely, and yet I craved more of him. Deciding that I would be more satisfied if I felt his heavy weight pinning me down into the bed, I reached for him with both hands and pulled him down to my body so he crushed me with his weight. It was hard to understand how Harry could fuck so hard without being vocal. But none of that mattered.

I was getting the sexual gratification I craved. And that was all that mattered.

"My love?" Jeremy called.

My response to him was a piercing cry as I exploded with pleasure, spilling my warm cream all over Harry's engorged cock. While I lay there trying to catch my breath, Harry detached himself from my body, letting me attend to my phone. I picked up the phone and laughed breathlessly as I watched my husband's cock ejecting a thick load of cum through his meatus.